"*The Baked Bean Kids* is fast-paced but full of detail. Its off-hand funniness is very appealing, and the text is matched by Derek Matthews's dynamic cartoon-style illustrations."
The Independent on Sunday

Ann Pilling is the author of numerous books for children, including *On the Lion's Side* and *Our Kid*, both of which were shortlisted for the Carnegie Medal. She also wrote *Henry's Leg*, which won the 1986 Guardian Children's Fiction Award. Originally from Lancashire, she now lives in Oxford with her husband, two sons and two cats.

Derek Matthews' illustrations have appeared in advertising, magazines and greetings cards, as well as in the *Teddy Bear Songbook* and other children's titles. He lives in Surrey with his wife and two boys.

1	2	3	4	5	6	7
8		10	11	12	13	14
15	16			17	18	
19	20			21	22	
23	24	25	26	27	28	29
30	31	32	33	34	35	36
37	38	39	40	41	42	43
44	45	46	47	48	49	50

☼ **Bigga's** ☼
Best Beans

SPECIAL
MINT
COLLECTION

		3	4	5	6	7
8	9	10	11	12	13	14
15	16				17	18
19	20				21	22
23	24	25	26	27	28	29
30	31	32	33	34	35	36
37	38	39	40	41	42	43
44	45	46	47	48	49	50

☼ **Bigga's** ☼
Best Beans

SPECIAL
MINT
COLLECTION

Some other titles

Art, You're Magic!
by Sam McBratney / Tony Blundell

The Finger-eater
by Dick King-Smith / Arthur Robins

The Haunting of Pip Parker
by Anne Fine / Emma Chichester Clark

Jolly Roger
by Colin McNaughton

A Night to Remember
by Dyan Sheldon / Robert Crowther

Pappy Mashy
by Kathy Henderson / Chris Fisher

Sky Watching
by Dyan Sheldon / Graham Percy

Tillie McGillie's Fantastical Chair
by Vivian French / Sue Heap

ANN PILLING

Illustrations by Derek Matthews

WALKER BOOKS

AND SUBSIDIARIES

LONDON • BOSTON • SYDNEY

First published 1993 by Walker Books Ltd
87 Vauxhall Walk, London SE11 5HJ

This edition published 1994

8 10 9 7

This book has been typeset in Garamond.

Printed in England by Clays Ltd, St Ives plc

British Library Cataloguing in Publication Data
A catalogue record for this book is
available from the British Library.

ISBN 0-7445-3183-7

Contents

Chapter One

~~Jocelyn~~
JOSS

The Baked Bean Kids were called
Joss and Pin. Joss had a round face
and stubby plaits. Her real name
was Jocelyn but she didn't like it.

It reminded her of glycerine, that sticky stuff which her mum sometimes poured into bubbling saucepans. Mum wrote cookery books and she was planning to be famous.

Joss didn't always like Pin. He was only little, but he was a big nuisance. He kept breaking her things.

One day she stuck a notice on her bedroom door:

Pin hated secrets, and Joss was
always having them. "My name's
Edward," he grizzled.

"No, it's not, it's Pin," she said,

11

and she wouldn't explain, except to her Very Secret Diary, which she wrote every night before she went to bed.

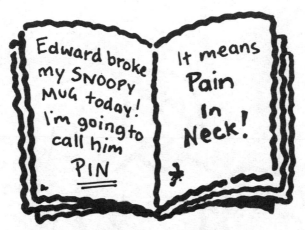

The secret diary
of Jocelyn Shufflebottom
(DO NOT READ)

Chapter Two

The worst thing about Pin was that he copied. When Joss got her new bike for her birthday he wanted one too.

I want one too.

When she got a kitten he wailed,
"Give me one." When the dentist
put a brace on her teeth he even
wanted one of those as well!

Then she started collecting things
– mugs and glass animals and
rubbers in funny shapes.

Pin copied, but he collected silly
things – the labels off tins, empty
cornflakes boxes and unbent
paperclips.

Joss was so fed up with Pin copying that she made an important decision. "I'm not telling anybody my plans from now on," she said to herself, and she wrote it in big letters in her Very Secret Diary.

But it was no use. Pin had this knack of finding out what she was up to and he found out about the baked beans. That's how the Shufflebottoms turned into the biggest bean-eaters this century.

Chapter Three

It started the day that Mum had a big shout. When she got cross her voice went all squeaky. It made Joss want to laugh.

squeak

"It's no good," she yelled. "The bath's full of old cornflakes packets, and the goldfish bowl's full of paperclips. In fact this whole house is bursting at the seams with useless rubbish," (squeak). "If you've got to collect things can't it be something little? And why don't you collect proper things?" (Squeak, squeak.)

squeak

squeak

squeak

Thinks

"You mean things I can keep for ever?" said Joss.

"Yes, for ever and ever," (squeak). "Now tidy up!"

Joss crept away and had a big think.

She started to tidy up Pin's bedroom. He was out, bouncing on Next Door's water bed. Tin labels: how boring, she thought, putting them in a neat pile.

Mum had said they should collect something little "that would last for ever and ever". But what did she mean? Buttons? Corks? Dried peas? Suddenly she stopped tidying. One of Pin's labels had caught her eye.

☀ Bigga's ☀
Best Beans

SPECIAL
MINT
COLLECTION

Absolutely free for only 50 of these labels

START COLLECTING NOW!

Joss started to read very carefully. She liked mints and Mum didn't let her eat sweets any more, because of her brace…

But it was nothing to do with mints. What you got for your fifty labels was a brand new set of coins, a penny, a five pence and a ten pence, everything, right up to a shiny gold pound. And none of them had ever been used.

Factory Fresh from the Famous London Mint, it said. You got a special book too, all about coin collecting.

Something little, that you could keep for ever and ever... This was the answer! They were doing a coin project at school and they were all supposed to bring "something interesting" to show the teacher. Joss folded up the beans label and put it into her pocket. One good thing about Mum's new cookery craze

was that she was always going
shopping. There'd be lots of tins of
beans in the food cupboard already.
She could just tear off the labels.

Oh, Jocelyn—
these are
wonderful. You
are so clever!

But there was a bad thing too; in
fact there were two bad things.
First, if Pin found out he'd copy.
Second, Joss didn't really like baked
beans.

Chapter Four

Mum didn't have any tins of beans. And when Joss asked her to buy fifty tins of Bigga's Best she said "No", just like that.

Big Ears Pin had sidled in from Next Door and heard every single word.

Can I get mints too?

"Of course you can, poppet," Mum murmured, dreamily stirring something in a pan. Joss felt like killing her. This meant one hundred tins of beans.

It was OK at first. She could manage beans on toast, baked potatoes with beans, beans and chips.

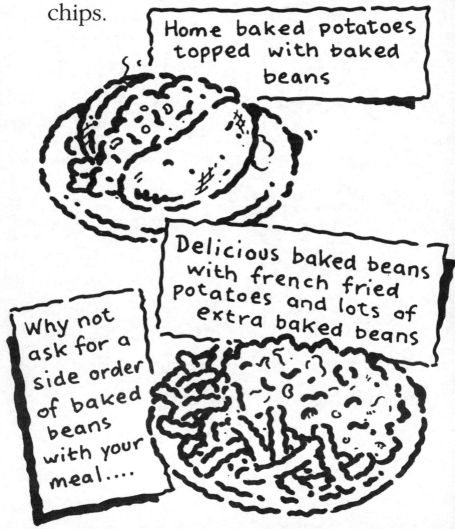

The labels began to mount up. Not fast enough though. When a new supply of beans arrived Joss tore a few labels off the tins. Mum went mad.

Toasted bread with lashings of baked beans

Also available without toast

"That's cheating," she said (squeak). As a result, for that day Joss got *peas* for tea.

"Serve you right," said Mrs Shufflebottom. "You can buy the next lot of beans yourself."

Joss did.

Next day she went straight down to Mr Banerjee's corner shop and bought three tins of Bigga's Best. The familiar red and yellow label was starting to make her feel a bit peculiar now, though. Every time she saw it her tummy seemed to puff up, like a balloon.

Mr Banerjee put the tins in a bag with a satisfied smile. He was fat – bigger than Mr Bigga, who did adverts on TV. "What's happening at your house?" he said. "Your mother's already bought six tins of beans this week. Is it for her cookery book?"

"Yes," Joss said. It wasn't, but Mr Banerjee had just given her a very good idea.

Chapter Five

"Why don't you write a bean cookery book?" Joss said to Mum, when she got home. Mum looked at her thoughtfully. Then she rooted among her recipe books and pulled out *Marvellous Meals With Mince.*

"You mean this kind of thing?"

"Why not?"

"All right. What shall we call it?"

"*Beans Give Me Burps,*" suggested Pin.

He wouldn't eat them any more,
but he still wanted his Special Mint
Collection. *Typical.*

"No, darling, I don't think so,"
said his mother.

Joss studied the mince book.

"Mmm... Not sure... I know,
let's call it *Bean Feast*. Short and
sweet." And she started scribbling,
straight away.

After that it was beans with
everything: bean soup, bean stew,
even bean sandwiches. These were
really awful. Joss tried to get rid of
them at school, but nobody seemed
to want any. So she stuffed them
behind the radiator.

That afternoon, in Projects, there was
a funny bean smell wafting through
the classroom. People started
coughing and covering their noses
with hankies. Hot fluff and beans
was a disgusting combination.

Chapter Six

Pin still refused to eat his beans up
and Joss told him she wouldn't give
him any labels unless he helped.
So he sprinkled some in Fred's
goldfish bowl.

The water instantly turned the colour of tomato soup. Then something peculiar happened. The goldfish normally did a sedate breast stroke, but after the beans he went mad and whizzed round and round. "He's doing the butterfly," said Pin.

Dad got worried. "He's only a little thing," he said, and he fished out all the beans with a spoon.

Every day Pin counted the labels
to see if they'd got enough. He
grew impatient. Next news was that
he'd fed some baked beans to the
cats.

Albert, the ginger one, was small
and timid; Victoria, the tabby, was a
great big bully. She pushed him out
of the way and gobbled the lot.

Very soon, though, she was
sitting on top of the shed giving
great howls, all swelled up like
something out of a monster book.

She didn't come down from the roof for two days and when Mum got the tin opener out she took one look at the red and yellow label and tore off, back to the shed. "She can read," Pin said proudly.

One morning Mum went off to London very early, to see a man about doing a new cookery book called *Great Puds of the Universe*. He absolutely hated baked beans.

Dad was in charge. "I'm on strike," he told the children. "I can't face another bean in any shape or form," and he got out the frying pan.

Joss gave her father a pleading look. "But we're nearly there, Dad," she wheedled. "We only need a few more labels. Do fried bread and beans, you love that."

"Not any more, I don't," Mr Shufflebottom said, cracking eggs. "I'm beginning to look like a bean.

The top of my head's growing to a point and I'm going this funny orange colour..."

Pin started to cry. "I don't want you to turn into a bean," he yelled. "I want my daddy! I want my mummy! I want my Special Mint Set and I want it now!"

Joss stormed off in disgust. She'd have her coins by now, if it wasn't for him cashing in. She pedalled off down to the shop.

Chapter Seven

MORE beans?

Mr Banerjee stuffed six tins of beans into Joss's bag, purring like a giant cat. "Sure you don't want another six?" he said. "Offer ends next Tuesday," and he pointed to the label.

Joss read it, then slunk off. She'd never get the mint sets now. She felt like crying.

Then a voice said, "Hey, Joss. Come 'ere a minute. Me 'n' Madge are starvin'. Wot you got in that bag then?"

It was Alfred, the old man who always sat on the wall opposite Banerjee's. He looked like someone out of the Bible, with his enormous grey beard and his long black coat. Madge was little and round, like a plump pink cushion.

Joss crossed the street and Madge
delved nosily into the shopping
bag. "It's only baked beans," said
Joss.

Wot you bin buyin, then?

"Hear that, Alf? Only baked
beans. This gel doesn't know when
she's well off. Baked beans is our
favourite. Hey, gel, do you think we
could..."

But Joss didn't stay to listen to the rest. Five minutes later she was in the kitchen at home, poring over Mum's *Bean Feast* recipes. This was the answer.

Chapter Eight

Alfred loved Mrs Shufflebottom's
bean soup; he slurped it down
greedily. And Madge was very
partial to bean curry. But the
biggest success was the bean
sandwiches. They actually asked
for more.

By lunchtime on Monday Joss
had got her hundred labels
and she posted them
off to
Bigga's
Beans by
Special
Express.

SPECIAL
EXPRESS

Bigga's Beans Ltd
Windy Way
Burpham
Wilts.

Next day she got a phone call. The labels had reached Bigga's Beans in safety and they could expect a surprise visit. Mr Bigga himself was to bring them the two mint sets. "Also," said the voice on the telephone…

There will be something else!

That night Joss couldn't sleep. Neither could Pin. Mr Bigga, the Beans Person, was all over the television. He didn't just sell beans, he did parachuting and deep-sea diving. He owned an island with palm trees.

"Perhaps he'll take me hunting sharks," Pin said, "or up in his helicopter. D'you think he will?"

No answer. Joss was trying to doze off. She wanted morning to come as quickly as possible.

At eight o'clock next day there was a loud knock on the door. Dad opened it to find a TV camera already filming. Next to it stood Mr Bigga. He was gigantic. So was the cigar he was puffing.

Pin and Joss were pushed forward. "Ah, the two lucky children," he boomed. "Allow me to present your Special Mint Sets. And your special coin books. Applause, please."

Mr Banerjee clapped politely, so did Madge and Alfred. Then Madge pulled at his sleeve. "'Ere, you've not got any of them beans going begging, 'ave you? Only I'm feeling a bit peckish."

"Dear lady," Mr Bigga said grandly, "stand aside if you please. It's time for the Something Else."

Pin and Joss couldn't speak for excitement. Pin was still hoping for a helicopter ride.

But four men in red and yellow
uniforms were busy humping
cardboard boxes into the front hall.

"What is it?" said Pin.

"Dear boy," said Mr Bigga, "as an extra special thank you to you all for the wisdom you have shown in buying my excellent product, I am giving you, at no extra cost, a year's supply of…

BIGGA'S
BEST BEANS!"

MORE WALKER SPRINTERS
For You to Enjoy